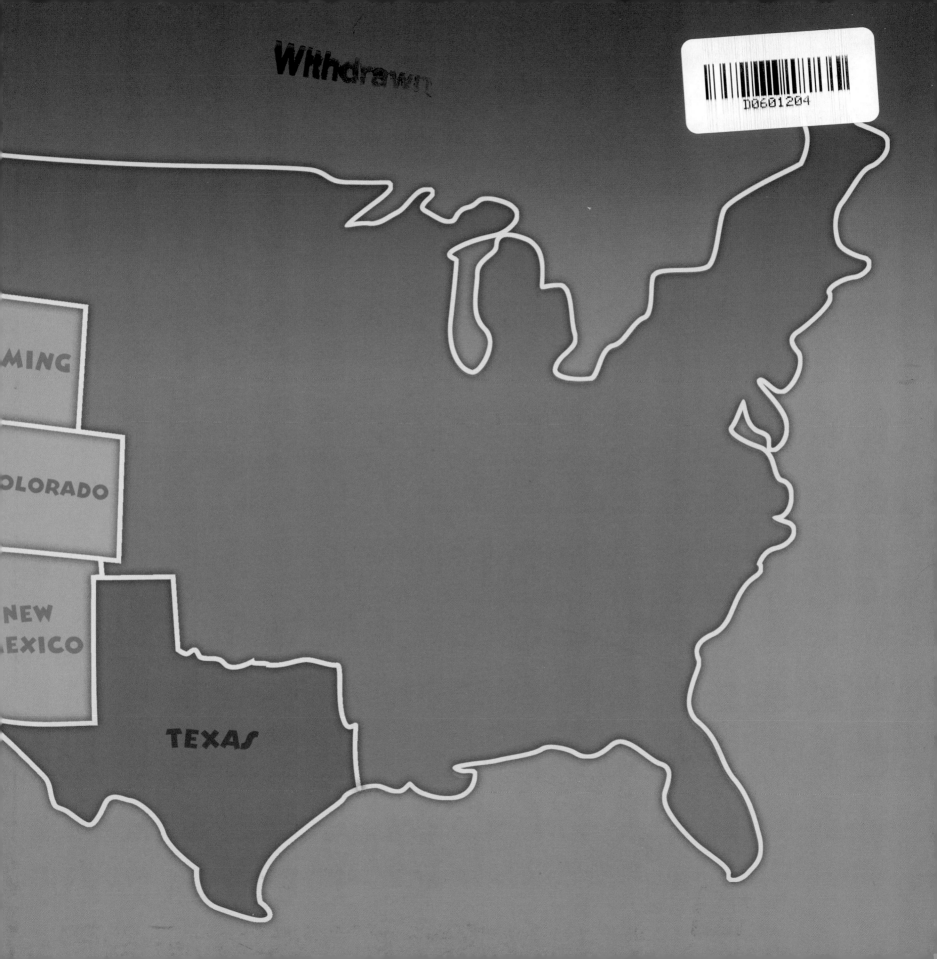

MING

OLORADO

NEW
EXICO

TEXAS

Text copyright © 2006 by Miles Backer

Pictures copyright © 2006 by Chuck Nitzberg

CIP Data is available.

Published in the United States 2006 by

Blue Apple Books

515 Valley Street, Maplewood, N.J. 07040

www.blueapplebooks.com

Distributed in the U.S. by Chronicle Books

First Edition

Printed in China

ISBN 10: 1-59354-134-1

ISBN 13: 978-1-59354-134-7

1 3 5 7 9 10 8 6 4 2

TRAVELS with CHARLIE
Way Out West

Miles Backer

Illustrated by Chuck Nitzberg

 BLUE APPLE BOOKS

You'll spy the Grand Canyon.

You'll find Jackson Hole.

You'll see Salt Lake City

and the Hollywood Bowl.

You'll spy Mt. McKinley

and Dinosaur Park

and a trail that was forged

by Lewis and Clark.

You'll see Carlsbad Caverns

and a ranch for old cars.

You'll spot Klamath Falls.

Can you guess where you are?

You'll spy a space needle,

a pineapple plantation,

and the great Hoover Dam

as you crisscross the nation,

following Charlie

wherever he goes.

He's off to the West.

Where is he?

Who knows!

Alaska THE LAST FRONTIER

STATE CAPITAL
JUNEAU

STATE FLAG

DID YOU KNOW...

- Alaska's state sport is dog mushing.
- "Nessie of the North" is the legendary giant trout of Lake Iliamna.
- Russian whalers and fur traders on Kodiak Island established the first settlement in Alaska in 1784.
- Joe Juneau's 1880 discovery of gold ushered in the Gold Rush Era.
- Alaska is more than twice the size of Texas and contains over half the world's glaciers.
- Juneau is the only capital city in the United States accessible only by boat or plane.

Where are the Northern Lights

in the sky?

Where's Mt. McKinley,

where you'll see eagles fly?

Find Anchorage, Fairbanks,

Juneau, and Nome.

Find a town called North Pole

and an Eskimo home.

Where's Charlie?

NORTHERN LIGHTS

St. Lawrence Island

NORTH POLE

Nome

Mt. McKinley

Barrow Eskimo Village

Nunivak Island

Yukon River

Fairbanks

Fort Yukon

Lake Iliamna

North American Championship Dogsled Races

Aleutian Islands

Anchorage

Gold Rush Museum

Kodiak Island

Yukon Route Railroad

Juneau

Fjords

Totem Pole Heritage Center

Ketchikan

Arizona GRAND CANYON STATE

Where's the Grand Canyon?

Where's an old copper mine?

Where's a meteor crater
and a petrified pine?

Find Flagstaff and Phoenix

and two reservations,

homes of the Apache

and Navajo nations.

Where's Charlie?

California *THE GOLDEN STATE*

Where's the Golden Gate Bridge?

Where's a beach? Where's a zoo?

I can find Tahoe

and Palm Springs. Can you?

Find San Francisco

and the Hollywood Bowl.

Find Napa. Find a surfer.

Find a tree with a hole.

Where's Charlie?

Colorado

STATE CAPITAL
DENVER

STATE FLAG

DID YOU KNOW . . .

- Colfax Avenue in Denver is the longest continuous street in America.

- The tallest sand dune in America is in Great Sand Dunes National Monument outside of Alamosa. It was created by ocean waters and wind more than one million years ago.

- Over 400,000 people ascend Pikes Peak each year, which is 14,110 feet above sea level.

- Mesa Verde features an elaborate four-story city carved in the cliffs by the Ancestral Pueblo people between 600 and 1300 A.D. The mystery of Mesa Verde is the unexplained disappearance of the thousands of inhabitants who created it.

- The Royal Gorge is the highest suspension bridge in the world, spanning the Arkansas River at a height of 1,053 feet.

Where's Royal Gorge Bridge?

Where's Dinosaur Park?

Where's Black Canyon,

a famous landmark?

Find the Colorado River,

flowing with trout.

Find Great Sand Dunes

and a moose camping out.

Where's Charlie?

DINOSAUR NATIONAL PARK

COLORADO RIVER

Denver

PIKES PEAK

WORLD FIGURE
SKATING MUSEUM
and HALL of FAME

Aspen

SKI SCHOOL

ROYAL GORGE
BRIDGE

Colorado Springs

LAKE ISOBEL

ARKANSAS RIVER

BLACK CANYON

PREHISTORIC
CLIFF
DWELLINGS

BALANCED
ROCK

GREAT SAND DUNES
NATIONAL MONUMENT

MESA VERDE NATIONAL PARK

ROCKY MOUNTAINS

Hawaii THE ALOHA STATE

DID YOU KNOW...

- The state of Hawaii consists of eight main islands: Niihau, Kauai, Oahu, Maui, Molokai, Lanai, Kahoolawe, and the big island of Hawaii.

- There are only 12 letters in the Hawaiian alphabet.
  Vowels: A, E, I, O, U
  Consonants: H, K, L, M, N, P, W

- The world's largest wind generator is on the island of Oahu. The windmill has two blades 400 feet long. They sit on the top of a tower twenty stories high.

- Haleakala Crater (Ha-lay-ah-ka-lah) is the world's largest dormant volcano.

- Hulope Bay is a marine preserve and is considered one of the best diving spots in the world.

- The island of Molokai contains the world's highest sea cliffs, Hawaii's longest waterfall, and the largest white sand beach in the state.

Where in the sea
can you stand next to sharks?

Where is Oahu?
Where's Volcano Park?

Find Lanai Plantation.

Find dolphins at play,

palm trees, Pearl Harbor,

and then find a lei.

Where's Charlie?

NIIHAU LIGHTHOUSE

HAULA FALLS

NIIHAU

KAUAI

OAHU

Pearl Harbor

Honolulu

MOLOKAI

LANAI

Lanai Pineapple Plantation

MAUI

KAHOOLAWE

HANAUMA BAY REEF

MAUNA LOA

VOLCANO NATIONAL PARK

Hilo

HAWAII

Rain Forest

Idaho THE GEM STATE

STATE CAPITAL
BOISE

STATE FLAG

DID YOU KNOW...

- Hells Canyon is the deepest gorge in America.

- Birds of Prey Wildlife Area is home to the world's most dense population of nesting eagles, hawks, and falcons.

- Pocatello is home to Idaho State University.

- In Idaho the law forbids a citizen to give another citizen a box of candy that weighs more than 50 pounds.

- Henry Spalding, a Presbyterian missionary, planted the first successful crop of potatoes in Idaho in 1837.

- Blackfoot is home to the Eastern Idaho State Fair.

Where's Lava Hot Springs

and historic Fort Hall?

Where is Sun Valley

where some skiers fall?

Find a trail that was forged

by Lewis and Clark.

Find Twin Falls and

Ponderosa State Park.

Where's Charlie?

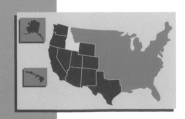

Nevada  THE SILVER STATE

STATE CAPITAL
CARSON CITY

STATE FLAG

DID YOU KNOW . . .

- Once the highest concrete dam in the world, Hoover Dam is 726 feet high and 660 feet thick at its base. 13,000 to 16,000 people cross the dam every day.

- Berlin-Ichthyosaur State Park is constructed around the fossilized remains of ancient, mysterious reptiles within a well-preserved, turn-of-the-century Nevada mining camp.

- Las Vegas has more hotel rooms than any other place on earth.

- Nevada is the largest gold-producing state in the nation.

- In Death Valley, the Kangaroo Rat can live its entire life without drinking a drop of liquid.

Where is Death Valley?

Where are palm trees?

Where's Pyramid Lake,

where a girl water-skis?

Find Carson City,

and Hoover Dam,

Las Vegas, Reno,

and a bighorn ram.

Where's Charlie?

New Mexico LAND OF ENCHANTMENT

STATE CAPITAL
SANTA FE

STATE FLAG

DID YOU KNOW...

- Each October Albuquerque hosts the world's largest international hot air balloon fiesta.

- The Rio Grande is New Mexico's longest river and runs the entire length of New Mexico.

- Tens of thousands of bats live in the Carlsbad Caverns. The largest chamber of Carlsbad Caverns is more than 10 football fields long and about 22 stories high.

- Elephant Butte Reservoir, created by a dam constructed in 1916 across the Rio Grande, is 40 miles long with more than 200 miles of shoreline.

- The Jemez Mountains are a volcanic field in north central New Mexico that overlies the west edge of the Rio Grande rift. These volcanoes are considered dormant but will probably erupt sometime in the future.

Where's the Santa Fe Trail?

Where's a rodeo ride?

Find Carlsbad Caverns,

where bats often hide.

Find a volcano,

dishes listening to space,

Los Alamos, and

a bird running a race.

Where's Charlie?

Oregon THE BEAVER STATE

STATE CAPITAL
SALEM

STATE FLAG

DID YOU KNOW...

- Crater Lake is the deepest lake in the United States and is formed in the remains of an ancient volcano.

- Oregon has more ghost towns than any other state.

- In 1858 the richest gold find in the Cascade Mountains was discovered in the Bohemia Mining District at Sharp's Creek near Cottage Grove.

- In 1880 a sea cave was discovered near what is now known as Florence. Sea Lion Caves is known to be the largest sea cave in the world.

- Tillamook is home to Oregon's largest cheese factory.

- The Oregon Trail is the longest of the overland routes used in the westward expansion of the United States.

Where are sea lion caves?

Where is Mt. Hood?

Where is a stage

where great actors have stood?

Find the Oregon Trail.

Find Klamath Falls.

Find the Pacific,

where a fishing boat trawls.

Where's Charlie?

Texas THE LONE STAR STATE

STATE CAPITAL
AUSTIN

STATE FLAG

DID YOU KNOW...

- More wool comes from the state of Texas than any other state in the United States.

- The state's cattle population is estimated to be near 16 million.

- Port Lavaca has the world's longest fishing pier. Originally part of the causeway connecting the two sides of Lavaca Bay, the center span was destroyed by Hurricane Carla in 1961.

- The Tyler Municipal Rose Garden is the world's largest rose garden. It contains 38,000 rosebushes representing 500 varieties of roses set in a 22-acre garden.

- More species of bats live in Texas than in any other part of the United States.

- Hot sauce is such an important condiment in Texas that there are annual hot sauce festivals and contests in most major cities.

Where is El Paso?

Where is Big Bend?

Where can you go

on a ride with a friend?

Find Amarillo.

Find a ranch for old cars.

Find the place where we send

NASA rockets to Mars.

Where's Charlie?

Utah
THE BEEHIVE STATE

Did You Know...

- The name *Utah* comes from the Native American Ute tribe and means people of the mountains.

- The people of Salt Lake City consume more Jell-O per capita than any other city in the United States.

- The National Cowboy Hall of Fame is located in Utah City.

- Levan is "navel" spelled backward. It is so named because it is in the middle of Utah.

- Belle Starr, one of the most famous women outlaws, is buried in an isolated grave southwest of Porum, Utah, near the Eufuala Dam.

- Utah has more man-made lakes than any other state, with over one million surface acres of water.

Where is Lake Powell?

Where is Mystic Hot Springs?

Where is the temple

where the Mormon Choir sings?

Find Salt Lake City,

the Bonneville Flats,

Sundance Film Festival,

and dinosaurs with hats.

Where's Charlie?

Washington THE EVERGREEN STATE

Where's the Space Needle?

Where's a great big whale?

Where's Puget Sound

and a place you can sail?

Find a volcano

without a top,

a museum for kites,

and a place apples drop.

Where's Charlie?

HOH
RAIN FOREST

OLYMPIC
NATIONAL PARK

SPACE NEEDLE

NORTH
CASCADES

COLVILLE NATIONAL FOREST

MONORAIL

GRAND
COULEE DAM

PUGET
SOUND
FERRY

Seattle

Spokane

MOSES LAKE
SKATEBOARD PARK

Olympia

WORLD KITE
MUSEUM

APPLE ORCHARDS

MT. RAINIER

MT. SAINT
HELENS

MOSES
LAKE

INTERNATIONAL
KITE FESTIVAL

BIGFOOT

FORT WALLA WALLA

Wyoming THE EQUALITY STATE

Where's the Platte River?

Where's Jackson Hole?

Find a man on a mountain

with a long fishing pole.

Find Flaming Gorge.

Find Devil's Tower.

Now find Old Faithful,

a geyser with power.

Where's Charlie?